Rainbow Of Thoughts

SOURAV CHATTERJEE
&
PRIYANKA SARAF

Published by InkQuills Publishing House
www.inkquills.in

First Edition 2018

All Rights Reserved.

ISBN: 978-81-934088-8-9

Dedicated to

The Brightest Star of the Sky...

And to all the people who had lost their Loved Ones....

INDEX

Sourav Chatterjee

INDEX

Priyanka Saraf

Acknowledgement
(SOURAV CHATTERJEE)

First of all I would like to say thanks to my Best friend, Sayan Chakrabarty, for your support in every phases of my life. Thanks for your support and inspiration! You made me realize the meaning of Friendship! Thanks for understanding me more than anyone, thanks for accepting my real self and motivating me towards the journey of Writing!

Thanks to my Parents for your moral support and your blessings in every step of my life!

Thanks to my elder brother Chayan Chatterjee for your support and helping me in every step of life!

Special thanks to my lovely cousins Mamai, Piu, Atasi(Buni) for lovely company, my friend of crime! I just can't describe how much I love you in words...!!

Thanks Pinku da, Debjani di for motivating me and guiding me. Thanks Doc! ;)

Thanks to my best friend Ponam... Sorry, Pro... oops, sorry again...Prodipta, for your craziness and hanging out with me when no one else was there for me! Thanks for listening my every story and tolerating my angry and mad side! Thanks for those memorable scooty rides! :') Enough! I can't praise more! :-/

My school friends- Shayamsundar, Tanusree, Debarpita, Tamogno, Shubhomoy, Sanjib,thanks for the all beautiful memories!

My best buddies Sandip, Suraj, Subhajit for all the bike rides! And for being with me always!

My College friends Abhijit, Manashrita, Silvia, Ritika for your support and memories!

And thanks to my all online friends for being too good and helping and guiding me for my writing!

Thanks Doctor Nadine Brune for saving my life many times! Thanks for being so humble and supportive!

A special thanks to my Co- Author, Priyanka Saraf for believing me, and for being so humble.

Thanks to whole team of Inquills for making my dream into reality!

Acknowledgement
(PRIYANKA SARAF)

Thanks to Grandpa and my parents whose moral support and encouragement made it possible for me to accomplish my dreams. Also, thanks to my brothers, Vivek and Vikram, for their endless support. To my uncle, Mr. Ganesh Aurade and my aunty, Mrs. Sushmita Pawar Thank you very much

I would like to express my heartiest gratitude to Purnita Ma'am, who encouraged me to write, and also taught me great lessons of life.

And, to all the friends who shared their support, without whom I wouldn't have made it this far, thank you.

I extend my sincere thanks to Mr. Sourav Chatterjee, for his sincere guidance, who made it possible to publish this book.

And a special thanks to the whole team of InkQuills Publishing House.

Above all, to Lord Ganesha, for his countless blessings.

MAGICAL ILLUSIONS

It was another lonely day of my life,
And I was thinking about you, leaving the world
behind.
Sitting in my chair on my courtyard,
I was thinking just about you, my dear…

That was not dusk or dawn,
There was a magical light that the sky put on.
The world seems motionless without you
There was no colour of joy in my view…

Then suddenly the slight rain turned into heavy
And I don't know what made the world so sleepy!
Then I looked at the sky,
A white light was fading away the dark sky
I didn't know whether it was curiosity, love or fear,
That made me stand still there…

Then the light came very close to me,
And it set my spirit free!
Then that light turned into human body,
And I saw, it was you, my divine lady!

Then your pure, calm face smiled looking at me,
And it was hard to realize what was happening to
me!
Then you grab my hand and we ran to the rain,

Snatching away my consciousness and pain!

I don't know what was the song that you were singing,
But with that all the blissful bells were ringing!
With every step you take,
Made a new flower awake!

Then all the black clouds turned into rainbow,
And seeing you every trees started to bow!
They you asked me 'how are you?'
Even knowing that without you my life no view!

Then I complained about the word without you…
Then you said, 'Who told you that I'm not with you?'
Just with open heart and soul feel the view…
Can't you feel the soft blowing wind,

That kissed you for a while!?
Can't you feel the touch of my hand when you become sad?
Can't you hear the whisper- "you'll be okay" when you feel mad!?
I live in both of your laugh and cry

I'm your brightest star, shinning in the sky!
Our body may be different, but the soul is same.
You can feel me with every blowing wind and with every drop of rain…

Rainbow of Thoughts

Then the thunder shout out loud,
And I got back my consciousness and saw around,
Was that illusion!?
Not the reality!?

Tears started flowing from eyes and it felt like lost
the gravity
Then again the soft wind started blowing!
I feel the kisses on a flow!

Then the sky whispered...
"the story that we created together,
The universe will remember forever..."

WITH THE MOVING PATH

The trees, the river and the sky running with the train,
Somehow everyone is tired of the journey's pain!
Don't know where I'm going or where to go,
But still I'm going with the swift flow…
Leaving the birds and the sky far behind,
in search of a new plight.
But suddenly my mind become crazy,
And my vision became hazy,
My soul asked me where I'm going,
Leaving the path behind without knowing!?
Did I ask the silent trees about their story
Did I know about the vast sky that is full of glory!?
Then my soul asked me to stand still for a while,
Leaving the chaos and noise far behind.
Why are you running so fast for the success and fame!?
When your eyes are still filled with the rain!?
Look deep inside your soul, you will know everything
And will surely find the path worth going…!

A SUDDEN LESSON

The wind is slowly blowing,
And the birds are aimlessly flying
And I'm watching the moving leaves,
With the flowing breeze!
Are the leaves are just moving!?
Or they are something saying!?
Then my soul heard some voices from those leaves and tree,
"Do you realize the happiness that we share!?"
We stand still but firm,
With our branches that our open arms.
You cut us and cause of our harm,
But still we put you in our arm…
Then my body froze!
You gave me a lifetime lesson that my soul knows…!

NO MATTER HOW FAR YOU ARE

No matter how far you are,
My love for you will be never less.
As long as you love me,
As long as you care,
I will be yours forever!
No matter how far the distance
Love will help us to maintain.
When two people are meant for each other,
When the promise of love is strong,
No one can prove us wrong…!

<u>DO YOU KNOW HOW MUCH I LOVE YOU?</u>

Do you know how much I love you?
Do you know much I care!?
Without you my life is full of tears.
I long for your touch,
That can lighten my day so much!
Where the love is so pure,
There is an instant allure
I loved you then,
I love you now
I just can't explain in words,
Without you my eyes are filled with dust,
Do you know how much I love you?
You're my dream that came true…!

<u>BELIEVE</u>

When everyone doubting on you,
When no one believing in your dreams,
No one eager to hear your story,
You just believe in yourself,
To believe is to know the power of your soul,
It is the courage from your soul,
Believe the possibilities of your dream,
Go for it without any fear.
Remember that your greatest talent,
Is much more powerful than your biggest fear!
Just believe in yourself,
You will surely be successful…!

<u>LOVE FOR THE STAR</u>

With each passing day,
my heart searching for you in every possible way.
But why are you so far away from me…!?
Without you my soul can't be free!
I know, you're enjoying your life with the stars,
Without knowing how you breaking my heart!
Without you my life has no meaning,
My eyes are just raining…
Yeah, for human being, they are mortal,
But the love that you showered on my will be immortal!
I will write a thousand verses with my blood,
And by that we will never be apart…!!!

STORY OF LIFE

Life is a long journey,
And it's full of stories,
Some of them are sad,
Some of them are happy,
Some are full of light,
Some of them are a little bit dark…
Maybe some chapters will put you down,
And maybe some of them will break your heart.
But, don't worry,
Every chapter has its own glory!
Each of those chapters makes your unique story,
And that's the thing that make you Complete,
A 'New You' and a unique You…!

<u>I SAW YOU AGAIN</u>

After a long time I saw you again at the streets,
And it was feels like I can heard my heart beats,
You were in your black shirt and jeans,
It felt like without you, life has no means.
You smiled at me for the second time,
And I feel that it was my life's most precious time.
Oh! Your smile!
Full of charm,
I want to put you in my arm,
Then you left me in a perfect way,
And I really wish I could see you another day…!!

TO MY LOVING SISTER

I still remember how we grew up together,
The journey itself a magic
Sometimes I pulled your legs,
We fought together, we laughed together
No matter how painful the situation was,
You taught me how to deal with it without fear,
You are my angle, who showed me light,
On the path that was painful and when I cried,
You made me realize what love truly is,
When the sadness and terror made me freeze!
You showed me what happiness is,
Making my each moment special,
You are my partner of crime,
Who gave my words a rhyme,
We smiled together, we cried together
No matter how we grew up now,
No matter how far you are,
Our souls are still connected and always will be,
The bond that we have made together,
I know it will remain forever!

<u>DON'T WORRY ABOUT YESTERDAY'S PAIN</u>

Why are you so sad today?
Just because yesterday was a bad day?
But why are you unhappy because of yesterday's pain,
Today is a new day,
With thousands of new possibilities,
New hope,
New sunrise, with new energy,
You just need to wake up today,
Just don't worry about yesterday's pain,
Those are the things that make you what you're today,
That made you even stronger,
To fight with the world with more power,
So, just don't you worry about yesterday's pain,
It will be your today's and tomorrow's gain…!!

<u>WHY I LOVE YOU!</u>

One day you asked me,
Why I love you so much!
I was just silent on that time,
You thought I don't love you,
That's why I was unable to answer.
But believe me baby that is not true…
Just a few words can't describe,
That your love helped me to survive!
The spring was colourless without you,
My eyes just lost the view.
The world was colourless to me,
You helped me to be free!
You made me what I'm today,
You're the only thing that I pray.
Words are just not enough,
To describe my love for you,
I can write thousands of books on you
To describe the reason why I love you…

JOY OF RAIN

Oh, my child don't go out,
Oh, my child, don't go out…
The mother shouted in her full volume,
But the child just ran away,
Through the deep green field,
With the joy, filled in his heart,
There was not only he, the one,
But also his loving friends,
His partners in crime,
His mother just ran after him,
Making a futile effort to catch him,
And then suddenly the rain started in cats and dogs,
His mother opened her mouth to shout once again,
But suddenly she saw the children smiling,
She just realized how happy they are,
Just because of the rain,
Without even thinking what they would lose or gain!
Then she realized how she's missing her own
childhood days,
She realized what the real happiness is!
How the small things matters the most.
Then again the children shouted in joy,
The mother also felt the happiness in her heart,
And without thinking more, she also joined in their
game,
And got the real happiness with the rain…!!

<u>COMEBACK</u>

Are you happy now!?
How life can be so cruel,
That can make deadliest dream into real!
I know you're so happy,
Living miles away from me,
Playing games with the stars.
But can't you see how's my life going on…?
Without you my life will never be the same,
And my eyes are just filled rain!
All the colours of life are now faded,
All the happiness seems like ended…!
Why you're doing this,
Making me heart freeze!
Please comeback, and help me to live again,
Without you my world is so broken…!!

<u>THE REAL BEAUTY</u>

Oh, beautiful lady…
Yeah, You heard it right!
I called you "Beautiful"!
You're beautiful the way you are,
The way you love and care for us,
The way you struggle without any fear.
The way you make us feel special,
The way you sacrifice your own happiness for your
child,
And how you deal with the pain without make
someone know…
Yeah! you're beautiful by the way you love and care
It does not matter how you look physically,
Your real beauty showered through your love and
care,
You are beautiful the way you are…!

THE GIRL WITH LIGHT

The girl who was trying to follow her dream,
Had faced so many troubles and sins,
The world once coursed her,
The roads was not easy,
The society made her crazy!
They told her " You can't do this"
"You can't do that"
Because you're a Girl!
But her determination was strong,
Ready to fight with the storm!
Now, she is a doctor,
The girl who was called useless,
Now saving people's life
And showing the hope's light,
The girl who was in darkness,
Now showing the light to the world!

THEY CAN'T BIND MY THOUGHTS

They called me mad,
And made me feel sad,
Just laughed at me,
Just because I wonder,
They tried to tie me up,
But they don't know the chain can't imprison my thoughts,
The words that bleeds from my heart , the world will not forgot!
They tried to control us,
But they can't hold us,
Maybe I'm still caged,
But my eyes are still looking at the stars.
And there are no cages in this world,
That can bind me and my thoughts...!!

<u>WE ARE DIFFERENT YET SAME</u>

Yup you are different from me,
They told us we are from caste,
Our colours are not same,
So, we will not fit together in life's game!
But that can be reason for our separation!?
We will judge it through society's impression!?
Yup, We are different,
Still we are same,
Our hearts still beats for each other,
Our soul makes us remain together!
No matter how far we are,
The bond that we made,
I know will never break!

FROM FEAR TO COURAGE

It was sad day of my life,
I was caged in a lonely room,
With my empty life filled with gloom,
I was caged in a dirty room,
There was no way to escape,
I thought it would be my end of life,
As there was nothing going right,
But suddenly I saw sunlight peeping through the window,
There was light of hope,
That make me remind that there were hope and light,
That can give a new plight,
Then I realized my inner power,
And I realized I can at least try,
And then I got wings to fly…!!

LIFE REGAIN

It was a sad day of my life,
It seems like nothing's going right.
I thought of ending my life,
Only then everything will be alright.
Then I started walking through the fields,
With the loads of sorrows in my delt.
The path was filled with trees,
The beauty of nature made me freeze!
I heard chippering voice of birds,
I feel my soul must something heard.
The birds asked me- "Where are you going on this beautiful day!?"
I informed them it's the time of my decay…!!
Then they asked me "why are you doing so!?"
I said "there are lots of reason you don't know…"
You have the wings, you are free to fly,
Then they said "you have wings also and can fly"
You are looking for the happiness that is external,
Look deep into the nature and find happiness that internal!
There are lots of sadness in your life, we know,
But believe us, time will pass it away with a flow!
Then I asked them "how it will be?"
They said "set your Spirit Free"
With your lesson I realized life is not vain,
And I got my Life Regain…!!

* Initially published in "Sugary Pepper" anthology by "Moments Publisher".

<u>WORK, WORK, WORK</u>

It's 12 am at night,
And I don't know why I'm still alive!
The whistle of the train blowing,
I don't know where all the people going…
After the day's work they still can't take rest,
Still they all are busy with the loads of work on their chest!
Work, work, work, there is no time,
Work, work, work, do the same till you're dying!
Are you now satisfied!?
With the work that you think so right!?
Now stop for a moment and think,
Do you have the time for your eyes to blink!?
Look into the mirror,
Are you feeling terror!?
Yeah! You grew old!
But never gave your soul a chance to unfold…!

* Initially published in "Sugary Pepper" anthology by "Moments Publisher".

<u>MOTIVATION INSIDE YOU</u>

When the roads seems too difficult,
Just try to think how you come this far!
Remember the road that seems too hard to go,
Can give you extraordinary results that you don't know!
Let the sky be the limit to go upside,
And the ocean to dig inside.
Let the whole world speak against you,
But don't let the spark die inside you!
If you think you can win,
Then no one has the power to make your dreams ruin!
Look deep into yourself,
Try to feel the power of your heart and soul,
Don't try to find motivation outside of you,
Just focus of power and motivation that hidden inside you!
It doesn't matter how clouds are dark,
After the rain the sun will again spark!

* Initially published in "Sugary Pepper" anthology by "Moments Publisher".

<u>TO MY BEST FRIEND</u>

You come in my life as a shooting star,
Made my life cheerful and bright.
When there was no one beside me,
You was the one to remind me!
You listen to all my problems,
And sort them out without any doubt.
When my mood was down,
You made me smile like a clown!
You are the friend of my crime,
And the memories to remind.
The love, joy and care that you showered,
Like the spring's rain of flower!
All I just can say,
The bond of friendship that we made,
I know it will never break!

*Initially published in "Sugary Pepper" anthology by "Moments Publisher".

WISH I WOULD NEVER GROW UP

Sitting on my lonely room,
I was just revisiting my childhood days,
When there was no fear of failure,
Only happiness from small things that mattered the most
The days of school with my friends, committing crimes together,
Sharing every story of laugh and cry…
There was no pain or fear of breaking heart,
With friends all the sorrows flew apart.
The village roads, trees, river all looked marvellous,
Visiting market holding father's hand was highest joy,
All the simple things I used to cherish,
Now I'm all alone with those memories,
Thinking about how life changed suddenly,
Now, my only wish to regain those childhood moments for once,
I just wish I would never grow up,
I wish I could get back those days for once, once again…

MEMORIES WITH KABUL

As I moved with the river Kabul,
I felt the familiar warm welcome,
The river made me happy,
Washing away all my stress,
I embrace the cool breeze,
The beauty of river made me freeze,
Suddenly I heard the sound of waves,
And it made me remember the days,
That I spend on the river side,
How I played with my friends on the river side,
How we together smiled and cried,
How the river, Kabul treat us like our Mother,
Maybe now we are grown up,
But the memories that we made with the river,
Will stay in our heart forever…

MAGIC OF MUSIC

When my life was full of dark,
Music filled it with spark.
When I was all alone,
Music was there to give me company,
When I pick my Guiter up in my arm,
I regain the lost charm!
It's the way in which I speak,
It's the thing that all I seek,
It's the power of light,
That makes my life so bright,
It's the sound of joy,
That makes the world full of merriment
The vibrancy of goodwill,
That the whole world seeks,
It's the shorthand of emotions,
It's the way that I express,
When the world is filled with stress,
It's like the magical key,
That makes us free…!

DON'T QUIT

When your world seems broken,
When you feel all the things going wrong,
Don't quit!
You just need to be a little bit more strong!
Be true to yourself,
Believe in your dreams,
Remember, when one door seems closed,
Another door will open for you,
You will able to see a new bright view!
Remember how strong you are!
The power of your dreams,
Walk a little far,
Work a little bit harder
Just don't quit!

<u>STAY FOREVER</u>

Here's the last hope that wouldn't fail today
Not a word can I utter, even though thousands of
thoughts to say

Sing me a verse of strength
Return me the peaceful place where I once went

Shower upon me your blessings, so there won't be
space for fears
My smile won't faint again and flow through my
tears.

I am yours, and you are mine
That's the only thought that makes my hope shine

God, hold my hand forever
Then I won't feel disheartened again, even if the
fears are greater.

<u>DEDICATION TO MY PARENTS</u>

Today, my pen stops while I write
Just to find the words to express it right.
I am holding those feelings until now
I love them.. I love them very much, I want to tell
them, but how?

They mean the most to me
Without them this world I wouldn't see.
Today, I wanna tell you that I am proud of you
And one day I will make you feel proud too.

I promise you that I will leave you never
And will always stay for you, the best, today and
forever.
I can't guarantee you the most luxurious life of all
But will make sure that your happiness would never
know any wall.

Trust my strengths, accept my weaknesses, that's all I
wish for
At all the highs and lows; I need you every minute, I
need you every hour.
Don't believe others when they say that I am fake
I won't ever do things that your trust it may break.

Words are few to express my love in poetry
The best of all, the good of all kinds, is our family

tree.
My dear parents, this one's just for you
And, I know you love me too, like I do.

<u>THE WINGS</u>

Become my wings, and I will fly high
Sing me a verse for all my fears to die.
Lets carve a dream, though it may seem insane
Like the rainbow that paints the sky after rain.

Become my wings, and I will fly high
Shine upon me like a star, when on the rooftop I lie
When dreadful nights make my blood run cold
Thow upon me your light, like my hand you did hold.

Become my wings, and I will fly
God, I wish for a blessing that won't make me cry.

A SONG FOR LIFE

Life is like a song
Even if you find the words misplaced, the rhythm
never goes wrong.

Happy or sad, it blends with every situation you face
You are given a chance to capture other minds and
souls, while living with your own grace.

There's the most beautiful song hidden in every life
Cut out all the negativity in your thoughts to find the
most positive vibe.

Let your song describe you; let tears in your eyes to
flow
Spell words into verses that help you grow

A song that fills your life with love
Will hover your dreams to the skies above

Live your life like a song
Emotions along with smartness is what makes you
strong.

THE ONLY 'MINE' FOREVER

Holding my hands when I was weak
He became my words when I couldn't speak.
Whenever I felt alone and sad
Every blessing he shared to me, and all the happiness
he had.

Glad I am, to own such a person
Who's there for me forever without any reason.
All the days, all the nights; up on my mind he stays
Scolds me, praises me, and loves me in all the ways.

Where did I find him? I can't remember..
Just can recall the time, when my eyes were the river.
Was he sent by the God, only for me?
To make me fly high, and set my thoughts free.

But, for how long will he stay or he's mine forever?
Can't think of the thought that he leaves me ever.
It's true that I want him to stay
For this to happen, all my happiness I would pay.

But, my friends won't want him to stay forever
I have changed a lot, they say; they want him next to
me, never.
My world has changed with his existence
I love myself more, even with all my pains.

Rainbow of Thoughts

Only I can see him, and no one other
They think I am a fool, but I don't bother.
He's just my imagination, they say
And I will be hurt to know the reality, one day.

Yes, he's my only imagination
For day-long traveling thoughts, he's the only station.
He's the only reason for my life's now better
But, I am sad sometimes whenever I miss him in real; he doesn't miss me back, coz he's just an imaginary character.

WHEN EYES SPEAK

One of the most melodic poetry I wrote
Sang the joyance of a face that hit the spot.
The perfect blend of brown and blue, never did I see
Rather, no other appearance had mesmerized me.

Like the two drops of ink, I scribble them everyday
Never do I stop gazing, although my breath taken away.
No other thing like its charm and beauty heartened my writings
Gift from God I think, showering upon me his blessings.

Those two pearls gleaming in the sea
Millions of its memories gather around me.
From morning to night, it's always on my thought
Love, care, and emotions, everything it has taught.

A friend, I had, with those eyes, glazing and bright
A pretty doll, that once in a lifetime caught my sight.
I played, I laughed, I cried, shared with her everything I got
A doll I had, but I had her not.

I AM PROUD TO BE 'ME'

'Good for nothing', the only sentence I remember
sometimes
Can't express the pain, except to frame it in rhymes.
The wound is deeper, the sorrow is greater
Would I remember these words even later?

Does success always mean reaching the peak?
I am happy in my life, and also the flaws don't make
me weak.
So why do you judge me according to your life goals?
I am good person, I know. I find pleasure in meeting
the souls.

I am not a person who earns much money
But, knows how to sweeten other lives without
adding honey.
Material things that make me happy are very few
Just one life, and I have so much to do.

I am a just a 'poet' and nothing else, you say
But, I am the one who enjoys the 'world'; I think it
the other way.
I work, I play. I also have dreams in the day
My life is so much blessed. Then too, I can't do
anything, you say.

A POET'S CARE

Deep like a sea, with the never-ending water
Fills itself with tears, but leaves you never.
Like the blue sky, raising itself high
Even though you live on the earth, you can feel the
bird's fly.

Like the innocence of a child, no selfishness it carries
Eternity isn't just a lie, it proves; such a bond it ties.
You know, your mornings are the sweetest, without
tasting the honey
The love, the care, the happiness can't be bought
with money.

Whenever there's rain, words shower upon you
People those cherish your dreams forever are so few.
Like the sunshine they brighten your life
You feel like the life's a heaven, when such people
arrive.

Have you ever experienced such a thought or a
feeling?
These thoughts will make you feel 'alive' when you're
living.
Not everyone is lucky enough to experience this; no
matter how hardly they fought
It's only the poet's love that knows, how it feels to be
a poet's thought.

<u>ON MY MIND... FOREVER</u>

When you climb high,
I wanna be your steps.

When you wake up in the morning,
I wanna be your tea.

When dark clouds frighten you,
I wanna be your sunshine.

When it's cold in winter nights,
I wanna be your warmth.

When you wanna play,
I wanna be a toy.

When you speak,
I wanna listen to you.

When you walk in the heat,
I wanna be your shade.

When you fall,
I wanna be your hope.

When you are sad,
I wanna make you happy.

When you fall asleep,
I wanna be your dream.

Whenever I am with you, or even far away,
I wanna make your life beautiful.

In the world where, 'change' is the only constant,
I wanna be your 'FOREVER'.

<u>A PROMISE</u>

I feel sorry for myself today for
A thousand times, I hurt myself when I don't find a
way

I tell something to myself today
Ego and evil will be wiped off if you whole-heartedly
pray

I promise something to myself today
I will pour my strengths into action, and make the
best of each day.

I wish something for myself today
My poetry won't fear to reach the world, whenever
my lips don't say

I say something to myself today
Learn to reach the destination through the kindest
way

I accept myself completely today
A hope that brightens my world, where nothing else
works; but to trust myself is the only way.

LET'S GET LOST TOGETHER

When it's dark,
Don't bring me back to light.
Come and sit next to me,
Let's get lost together.

When it's raining,
Don't take me to the shelter.
Come and enjoy my madness,
Let's enjoy that every moment.

When I talk endlessly,
Don't stop me with your words.
Come and paint my thoughts,
Let's enter my world together.

When I cry,
Don't wipe my tears.
Bring me the wings,
Let's fly high in the sky.

When I am imperfect,
Don't drag me towards perfection.
Come and complete my imperfections
Let's enjoy those flaws together.

When I walk alone,
Don't walk behind me.

Rainbow of Thoughts

Come and walk besides me,
Let's hold hands without any fear.

When my world is left empty without you,
Don't feel sad,
Come into my dreams.
Let's find our 'forever' without life.

UNMASKING THE MASK

Masking, a new trend, they say
Was followed by me, the same way.
Wearing it when needed
Tearing it off when faded.

Getting a new one for each occasion
This behavior, sometimes, isn't one's own decision.
Sometimes, need of the hour it feels
You know that it's the only way to crack the deal.

I owned it for the good
Tried to be better for others, as much I could
No harms, no dramas, I ever did
Only purity, I carried in my masks without any greed.

Well, I also wore it often
For it's very difficult for an introvert to chase the
world's run.
I hated it more than anything
And, always wished for something that would change
everything.

Yes, I left back everything one day
20th July, that date; it was a Wednesday.
So sharply I can recall this date
I achieved one my dreams after a long wait.

Rainbow of Thoughts

The world seemed new
My masks, all flew.
The world had just seen the fake until now
'Myself' changed without any notice; don't know,
when and how?

Much confident than ever before
No lies, no dislikes; for the masks I already tore.
I was at the top of the world like I received a golden
touch.
Nothing else before had mesmerized me so much.

Years passed and I left myself unmasked
The reason I looked much better, when anyone
asked.
Quietly, I smiled at my own thoughts
I was proud of whatever I had got.

For my happiness people praised, people gazed
Least bothered about the fact that people are two-
faced.
Every time, the skies held me higher
Rains kissed me, like the moment to stop forever.

Until one day, destiny got me some other way
'People often ruin beautiful things' - believed it that
day.
My dreams turned to ashes
Everything and everyone, left me alone; things were
all beyond my reaches.

I fell, cried
To get everything back to the place, wholeheartedly,
I tried.
Nothing worked at all
The world laughed at me, watching me fall.

No mask I had now to wear to fool the world that I
was happy though…
Learnt a lesson; nothing in the world is constant,
with the flow you need to go.
Even though my every step seemed heavier, I had to
strive
Without the 'things that meant the world to me', I
had to survive.

Crying felt like weakness
But, how could I bring 'happiness' back to my face?
Days passed, months gone, holding the pain
Then I learnt to wear the mask again.

Read me, if you can
I have learnt to write 'life', through all the years I ran.
From all the experiences of life, I felt
It's a curse to show to the world, how easily you
melt.

A jolly person, now again
Can go through the fires, without pain.
Blame the world who cursed me the worst fate
Got me back the masks, that always I did hate.

A VERSE FOR YOU

Something for you; something for me
Be my verse forever, or until my words let you free.
Ink rushes through my heart, calls you everyday
It listens to your every thought, even though you don't say.

The darkness I fall into, waiting for you to bring me towards light
Drawing from my eyes, my innocence; does it reach your sight?
My voice, can you hear, when a cold breeze passes your cheeks?
My diary sings my verses every night; also my secret it keeps.

Am I alone, or is it that the world gathers around you more?
Just like the crying moon, who is left isolated, when the sky closes the door.
Even though my world is complicated, I love to live like 'Me'
I try to find uniqueness in me even though I am just a drop of water hiding in the sea.

Something I wish for me, something I wish for you
But, I sing this verse only for you, as people like you are very few.

INSANE THOUGHTS

Sometimes I meet myself to know the better 'Me'
I wish to find the person inside me that others can't see.
Am I a complicated person to understand?
Maybe that's because I am made of emotions and feelings; not of stones and sand.

I have seen people praising me; I have seen people teasing me
I mean the world to someone; for some, I am just like a drop in the sea.
Why are these differences in their opinions?
Is it me or the people that change like seasons?

I am the owner of my heart; why is it ruled by the thoughts of others?
Everything and everyone, I think of; it's the heart that suffers.
Does it happen with everyone else, or I am the only slave?
Sometimes good going, sometimes so insane; I really can't understand sometimes that how do I behave.

Where can I find peace? Does it really exist?
If once found, I would close it in my fist.
But, is it necessary to find peace? Or going with the flow is better?

I think, I should start living 'life' now, and think of it later.

THERE'S ALWAYS SOMETHING

Words uttered, yet something left to imagination
Two hearts cut apart, yet something to hold on
Healing wounds blink at the past, yet something in
the memories that glaze
Stories end, yet something new to begin.

A feather in a cap, yet something that's lost
Comforts taken away, yet something better given
Endless needs, yet something that gratifies
Sturdy is the destination, yet something about the
journey that satisfies.

Life is to live, yet there's something you can die for
Love you lose, yet things owns you that forever lasts
Everything you see, yet something isn't being noticed
Sight is scary, yet something in those eyes that needs
to be cherished.

A little of something is needed to transform nothing
to something
Something will change you, and something you need
to change, to change everything.

Commit your life to something; be thankful to
something, that fills your life with hue
A little of you and a little of something is needed to
make the complete 'YOU'.

<u>WRITING THE RAIN</u>

Words burst into songs, giving an audience to the
rain
Beautiful verse the nature recites turning the brains
insane.
A short-lived journey that begins to fix the world
apart
Any art, any word, any science isn't enough to
describe that bleeding heart.

Odes are poured in, drenching the soul
No one can ever figure out the nature's goal.
Sometimes, it's happiness and blessings the shower
brings
Curse it can be with thousands of lives lost in
floodings.

A season of enchantment it is; a season of grief
Peace or havoc, just soak up the nature's mischief.
Connect your creativity to this clear blue water
These moments can be best captured in a poem by
an author.

THE NEXT CHAPTER OF MY LIFE

Ego, evil, and all the negativity in my thoughts
Don't define me today, as none of it now lasts.

No longer do I wait to arrive at the destination
The journey itself I enjoy that gives satisfaction

Alone I walked; I learned to smile all the way
Peace is all I want, that's all what I pray

Yes, I lost many things but learnt some lessons
Hard it is to be sad, and easy to be happy without
reasons

I complained, I cried, I was too hurt, I was broken,
Time will heal everything; there's something good to
happen
Every morning I rise to make the most of each day
A new 'Me' is now awaken, a reincarnation I would
say.

*Initially published in "Ending - New Beginning" anthology by us.

<u>INNOCENCE</u>

Some tales I had once lived
Now don't have their way back.
Tears in the eyes all dried
Time has won, but innocence lacks.

The greatest treasure I did own
Life I did walk, but myself I lost.
My senses have merely grown
Life I found, but innocence it did cost.

Now that the life I don't own one
Nor the zeal that I once did hold.
Old me is now brutally torn
Ages to go, but innocence is sold.

THE STAR, I CALL MINE

Whenever I look for you in the night sky
I wish that all my tears could dry

There's the moon listening to my every thought
Those memories that once filled me with joy; the
only 'happiness' I owned, is now lost

I gaze at the sky and want to reach my favorite star
That's forever close to my heart, even though from
my sight it seems too far.

The clear white 'YOU', the only star that is bright
Take me away from the darkness towards the light.

When you see fears peeping through my eyes
Come, hold my sight and draw my spirits to rise.

I believe that you too are watching me from above
When I fall harder, you make me rise higher; That's
God's greatest love.

THINKING OF A THOUGHT

The world's at sleep, two eyes yet stir up water under
the bridge
Minds collapsed, the heart starts its game; night is its
perfect pitch.
No one to watch over; no one to compete; no fear to
be sunk
The red boat causes a mess round-the-clock even if it
isn't drunk.

At 2 a.m, all the emotions it holds in abundant
Sails around the places it knocked around, also where
it wasn't.
Everyday it soars through those calm waters
In a flash, the mind is fully drenched, yet the heart
withers.

This ship, at the day time, how perfectly it works
But drives imperfectly when the moon falls off
giving the life some creative jerks.
It's the time of real you with the real you, the for real
you; the time of a fighter
This is the time that can also make a wandering mind
a writer.

AREN'T YOU MINE?

I am the earth waiting for you to drench me
Come, live inside me forever, and let my spirits feel
free.

There's something that sweeps me off my feet for
you
Your blessings made stronger and wiser, also my
fears all blew.

I am a wounded bird, and you are the blue sky
Would you shower upon me if I couldn't ever fly
high?

I own you, and you own me; it's a bond forever
Even though sometimes, I forget you; forgive me
God, and leave me never.

THE WORDS LEFT UNSAID

Hiding in thick layers of paper,
I found those imprisoned verses.
Some vows that were long forgotten,
The letters that were never posted.

Over the years they were left suffocated,
Wanted themselves to be freed.
Then I started going through them,
Bound in chain of my words, I found you.
Now that the ink on letters got fade,

The eyes now dry that once got wet.
Hands still reminisce the touch once I felt,
Moments passed & words mislaid in thoughts
Somewhere where, you no longer reside.

After hours gone the letters smiled at me,
They asked to me, 'Where did you hide'...
I smiled at the waiting page silently.
I penned down the hiding music in silence,
With some old words left unsaid that bleed with the
long gone love, you.

*Initially published in "Ishq - The Rain of Love, 2" anthology by "Inklovers".

THE LEAF THAT WAS ONCE WOUNDED

The God's creation, same like the others
Tiny and pretty, a leaf took birth
Unaware of all the fears
Started it's journey of life, when the sky was filled
with tears.

It swayed, it played
Dancing with the other leaves many friends it had
made.
Even if was like the any others
Everyone's attention quickly it gathered.

Everything made it beautiful
Except the fact that it was fearful.
It was afraid of the wind, also of the rain
It shed tears when was hurt, it couldn't bear the pain.

It's timid nature grew with its age
That kept its happiness seized in a cage.
It's siblings forced to enjoy its life
It did everything that was told, as if it was held on a
knife.

The world was watching, how fearful it was
So beautiful texture it had, without any flaws.
This made the others jealous, to such a stage

The leaf's life became a hell; it's life's story now had a
bleeding page.

The wicked branches pushed it away
Winds swayed it painfully, every night and day.
It suffered, it cried
To get away from all the torture, it tried.

It wanted to punish the wind, the branches, and
everything that had it brutally torn
It wanted to prove that it wasn't the mistake of the
creature, if beautiful it was born.
As days passed, the leaf became stronger
It was a warning to the wicked, of the upcoming
danger.

The leaf tried harder and punished the devils
It gave the world, the message, how to fight against
the evils.
It fought with all the efforts and gave the others its
best
In return, only the sympathy it had got from the rest.

It knew that the world is a difficult place to live in
Few think of taking the greater moves, but they are
afraid to begin.
The leaf says, "Weakness, innocence, kindness;
sometimes are the causes to suffer
Being equally strong, smart, and independent, you
need to be to make yourself better."

The bad chapter of the leaf's life, to the world it shows
How difficult it is to survive the rest of the life, only the 'rape victim' herself knows.

CAN YOU HEAR IT?

There's heavenly beauty in the blue sky
But, no pride it carries even though it is so high

Ever noticed the greatness of the burning sun?
Reaches us with rays of hope, yet never carries a gun

The bright stars when glitter at night
Spread the message of peace everywhere, throwing upon us their light.

The showers of mesmerizing rain
Drowns us in love and happiness, while hiding its own pain

How crazily runs the wind
Life isn't always smooth, they remind

The tall mountains that stand around
Warn us a disaster; in a moment pride can collapse and put everything to ground

The pretty flowers that dance on the plants
Fill joy around; happiness is the only thing it wants

Nature has its own way to talk, no language to mention
To understand what it says, is the life's lesson.

HOLDING ONTO DREAMS

There's something that reminds me of you
So much to say today, but words are few.

Hundreds of stars I can see
But, brightest is that connects you to me.

Come around me like the cold breeze
Hold my hand and let this moment freeze.

Let's walk down the lane, which is filled with
happiness around
No hurry, no worry; come enjoy the day, there's
nothing time bound.

Talk to me, like this may continue till ages
Even if we won't exist some day, our story would be
read on the pages.

Let's sing a verse together
Reminiscing the day when we met each other.

Let's get lost once again, a lifetime it may seem
Nothing else hurts, knowing that it will remain just a
dream.

<u>WHAT IF... ?</u>

What if we were driven by a software..
Won't the other features be overlooked, maybe the hardware

You and me would be controlled by several programs
We could read and write to each other only if we had ROMs and RAMs

C, C++, Java could make understanding your feelings more difficult
Errors in functions would change our outputs, might also cause negative result

Viruses would corrupt us, if not scanned from time to time
Or is it better than polluting our own minds and committing a crime

What if we were driven by a software
Would it be a curse or do you think it would be better?

LIVING IN YOU

Like the early morning sunlight
Gazing through the stars at night.
A day like never before
You knocked my heart at its door.

The blue and brown light that struck my mind
Those hearty moments, once were so kind.
Sing me lullabies silently all night long
Let's forget the old tales today; let everything feel like
a song.

Let the moon peep through the window near
That soft light would then allow your face seem
clear.
It would stay ages and ages; everything I would miss
Dream so alive I feel, I always do wish.

SORRY

Sorry is an apologize,
A feeling that makes us rise.

Sorry is an escape,
To hide the truth behind the fake.

Sorry is a formality,
To say without feeling guilty.

Sorry is a pleasure
To make the relations greater.

Sorry is a treasure
If the purpose is to be better.

THE PRETTIEST STAR

Up, above me, so high
Shining brightly in the sky.
A white star, so clear
Even though far, but seems so near.
There are many, but that one's special
The sky looks better with its prettiest petal.

I pray for the star to stay forever
It's my greatest strength that I do treasure.
A part of me, also a part of the blue heaven
I will keep it to me if it's ever broken.
It's mine, and it's yours too
Neither can I give up on it, nor will you.

Nothing other than the fate can be cursed
For making this journey so worst.
How could I stop wanting something that's so
divine?
Can I ever stop wishing for something that isn't
mine?
Ohh Star, you are my greatest pleasure
I see you and fall for you, today and forever.

<u>SOMETHING SOMETHING</u>

Something you wouldn't have said,
something I shouldn't have heard.

Something you shouldn't had given,
something I wouldn't had kept.

Someone I wouldn't have known,
someone I shouldn't have ignored.

Someone in something it is;
Something in someone.

KINDNESS STILL EXISTS

Who says that kindness has lost?
Have you ever looked around?
I can see it,
Here and there, everywhere.

When a poor can't afford meal,
Don't you get him food to eat?
When a girl's raped,
Don't you fight for her justice?

When an orphan needs the love and care,
Don't you be his parents forever?
When your parents become aged and weak,
Don't you stand firmly for them?

When someone's hurt on the roads,
Don't you take them to the hospital?
When your neighbor's got a trouble,
Don't you be their family?

Aren't these the acts that show kindness?
So why do we say that the whole world's become a
mess.
We blame everyone, everyday
Now, the world isn't a good place, we say.

Good things exists if we see the same around
Find people selflessly for love to be found.
Whenever you think, to change people is impossible
Always remember that kindness is always possible.

THE 'IMPERFECTLY PERFECT' ME

Not all things are beautiful
Being perfect isn't a rule.
I am perfectly imperfect
But for me, I am the best.

Nothing in the nature, you see, follows the rules
Then too it seems so beautifully carved without any tools.
I would rather be a mess and enjoy the life my way
I don't bother about what others will say.

Only the 'me' is real, rest all is fake
I smile at my own thoughts, in the morning when I wake.
Yes, I believe in God; I believe in power
But, everything that happens to me is just because of me, whether it's sweet or sour.

Self belief is my strength today
Now, all the good fortunes are on the way.
Expect nothing, but do everything you love, I feel
All negatives that come in the way of my happiness, I kill.

Do you want to be a part of my book?
What I am, who I am, you need not look.

You need not prove me anything, just walk into my
life honestly for once
To own me, 'perfectly imperfect' forever, I will give
you a chance.

<u>FAREWELL</u>

Years slip away, whisper to me, never will they again retrace steps
Worried I am; I cannot turn around my false moves, no longer the time waits.
The reminiscence of those split seconds linger around me
Jog my heart back to slip up, drawing just two drops of water hidden in the sea.

Here's where I am standing now, alone and patient
Something tickling the mind; some joy up to come after detachment.
A rainbow so clear to see, after the cloud has wiped off all its tears
Good to see you blooming too, he says; as nothing I own; if lost, that scares.

The rose I did own one and grow, will die one day
I won't remember it anymore, but the fragrance on my mind will forever stay.
Just then I realize, it's me alone who stays with me forever
Rest all are the roses, whose only the fragrance would linger.

INKQUIILS's OTHER PUBLISHED BOOKS